THE MONSTER WHO ATE DARKNESS

JOYCE DUNBAR   JIMMY LIAO

WALKER BOOKS
AND SUBSIDIARIES
LONDON • BOSTON • SYDNEY • AUCKLAND

Jo-Jo couldn't sleep.
He didn't like the darkness
under the bed.

He thought a monster might
be hiding there ...

well ...

this time ...

there WAS!

A tiny speck of a monster,
so small he could hardly be seen.

But he had a big empty feeling inside him
that made him hungry, very HUNGRY!

He nibbled at a woolly slipper
under the bed.
Ugh! Horrible!

He bit into a tin toy car.

Ouch!

It hurt his gums.

Then he saw

something interesting.

It was a box.

He peeped through a pinhole in the box
and saw that it was full of darkness.

He sucked the darkness out of the box, every last bit.

Delicious!

The monster was
a teeny bit bigger.
And he was
still hungry.

He looked around for
something else to eat.

There was a lot more darkness under the bed.

The monster ate all of it.

He licked into the darkest corners

until there wasn't any left.

The monster got quite a lot bigger.

But he was still hungry.

So he ate all the darkness in the cupboard and all
of the darkness hiding behind the folds in the curtains.

The monster
got **bigger**
and **bigger.**

But he was still hungry.
So he slipped out
of Jo-Jo's house ...

and went looking in all the other houses

for more darkness to eat.

He found darkness in cellars.

And attics.

And chimneys.

He ate it all up.
He licked them
quite clean.

He found new and exciting ways to eat the darkness.

He liked darkness as spreads on burnt toast.

He liked darkness sandwiches.

He especially liked darkness soup, which he made out
of the darkness at the bottom of wells. And darkness
stew, which he made out of the darkness in ditches.

Then he found rabbit holes –
he ate all the darkness there –

and foxholes –

a real delicacy.

And then he found
the darkness in caves.
There was so much of it
but he scooped the caves
out and scraped
them clean.

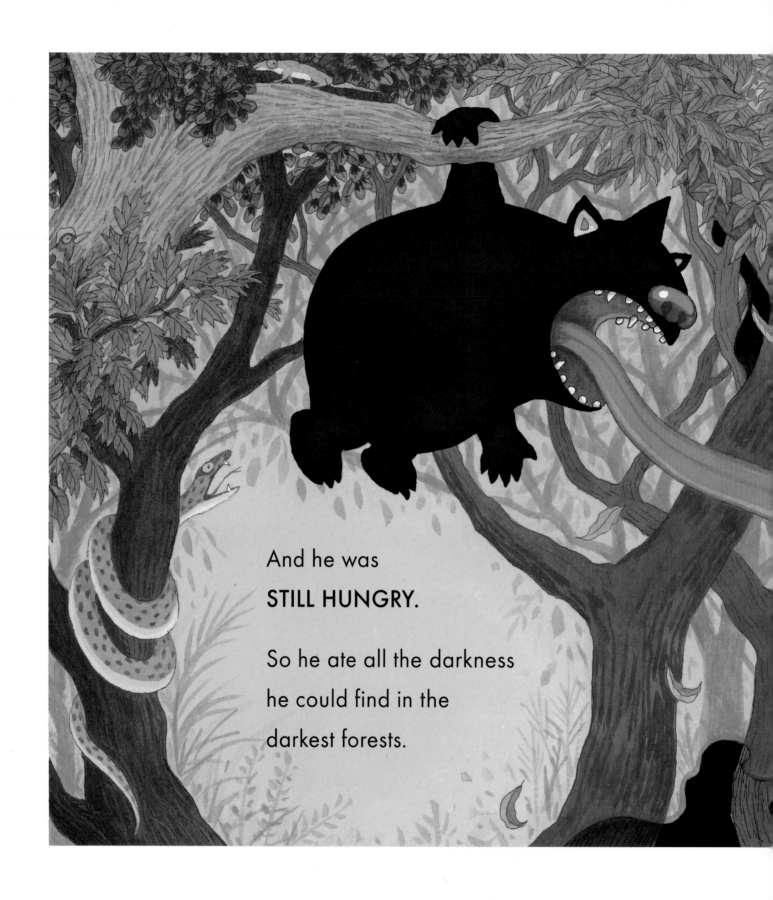

And he was

STILL HUNGRY.

So he ate all the darkness
he could find in the
darkest forests.

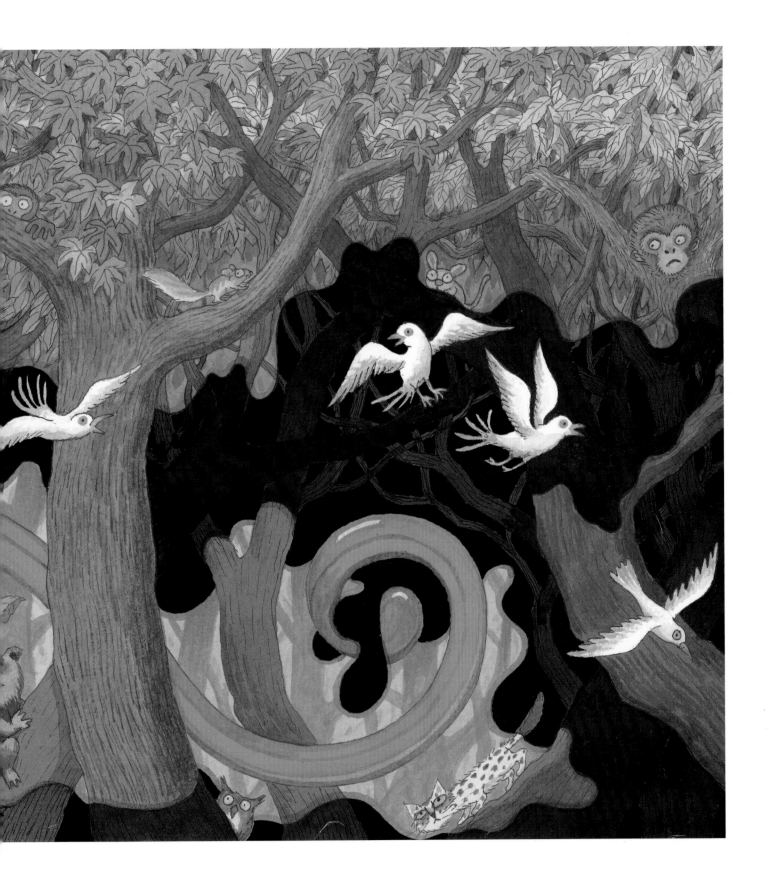

And all the darkness
at the bottom of
deep volcanoes.

And though
the monster
got bigger
and
bigger ...

he was **STILL HUNGRY.**

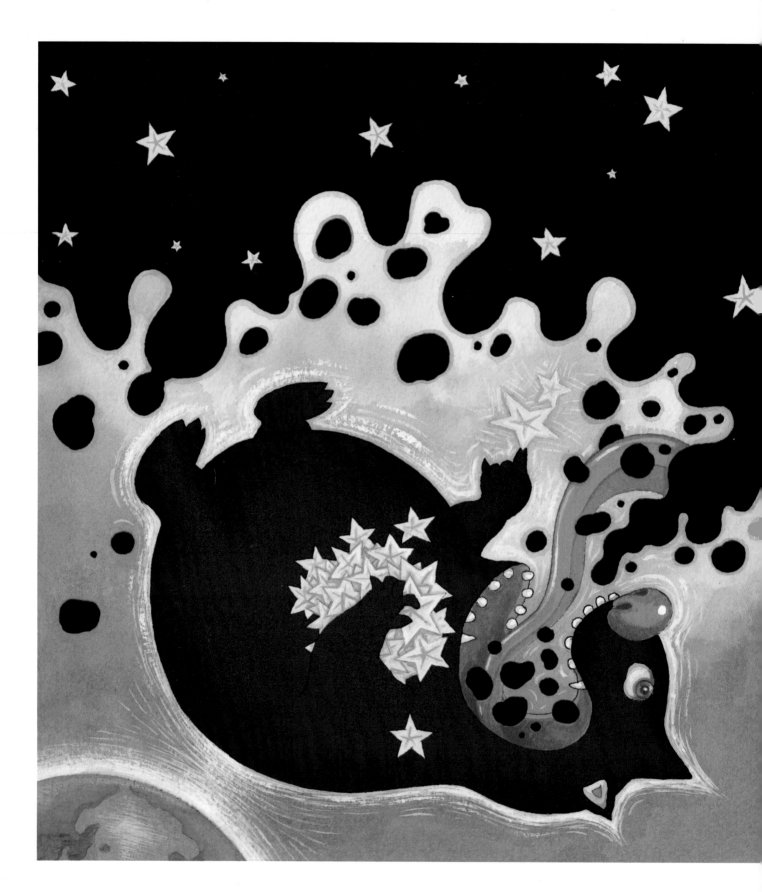

He was afraid that that he had eaten

all the darkness there was.

Then he saw the night coming.

I'm sorry to say, he ate

ALL THE DARKNESS OF THE NIGHT!

He ate it all the way to the moon,

which no longer shone in the sky.

He ate it all around the stars, which no longer twinkled.

Now there was no more darkness.
There was no dawn and no dusk.
There were no shadows and
hardly any dreams.

There was only the light.
The stark and staring light.

The monster sat on a lonely planet
feeling very sad that there was no
more darkness for him to eat.
He looked at the earth.
The earth looked very sad too,
even though it was shining bright.

You see,
without the dark,
the owls didn't wake
up at night. They slept
so long and so soundly
they kept falling out
of their treetops.

Fireflies didn't bother
to go out because
they couldn't be seen.
Cats' eyes no longer
shone so the cats
lost a lot of
their glamour.

Hedgehogs went stumbling about blindly in the
night-light and kept bumping into each other.

Foxes crashed into boulders.

Bats hung the right way up
instead of upside down.

Bears were equally upset
and confused.

Then the monster heard,

from far away, a strange sound.

It was a little boy called Jo-Jo, crying.

He was crying because he couldn't get to sleep.

Why couldn't he get to sleep?

Because there was too much light.

WAAAwaAwawaAaaaa

Even though the monster was so
big and so full of darkness, he could
squeeze into the smallest spaces.
He could slide through cracks in
windows and seep through
pinholes in boxes.

So he crept back to Jo-Jo's bedroom.
He saw the little boy crying for his
mother, who didn't hear him
because she was huddled under
the bedclothes, trying to
find some dark.

Then the monster did something amazing.

He picked up the little boy in his great dark
arms, which were very soft and not a bit hairy,

and he rocked him as if he were in
a cradle. And he hummed a darkness lullaby.

Soon Jo-Jo was asleep. So was the monster.

He wasn't hungry any more.

He just didn't have that big empty feeling inside him.

Instead, he snored and snoozed,
with the little boy safe in his arms.

And as he snoozed,
all the darkness oozed out of him.

It went right back to where it belonged.
It oozed and it oozed until the monster
was no more than a tiny speck again.

A small, happy speck

ıst asleep in the arms of a boy!

For Joe Dawes ~ *Wood Carver*
David Holgate ~ *Stone Carver*
J. D.

First published 2008 by Walker Books Ltd
87 Vauxhall Walk, London SE11 5HJ

This edition published 2009

2 4 6 8 10 9 7 5 3 1

Text © 2008 Joyce Dunbar
Illustrations © 2008 Jimmy Liao

This book has been typeset in Futura T Book and Futura T Medium

Printed in China

British Library Cataloguing in Publication Data:
a catalogue record for this book is available from the British Library

ISBN 978-1-4063-1554-7

www.walker.co.uk